Nora Bone and the Tooth Fairy

Brough Girling and Tony Blundell

Collins

Best Friends · *Jessy and the Bridesmaid's Dress* ·
Jessy Runs Away · **Rachel Anderson**
Changing Charlie · *Clogpots in Space* · **Scoular Anderson**
Ernest the Heroic Lion-tamer · **Damon Burnard**
Weedy Me · **Sally Christie**
Something Old · **Ruth Craft**
Almost Goodbye Guzzler · *Two Hoots* · **Helen Cresswell**
Magic Mash · *Nina's Machines* · **Peter Firmin**
Shadows on the Barn · **Sarah Garland**
Clever Trevor · *Nora Bone* · *Nora Bone and the Tooth Fairy* · **Brough Girling**
Private Eye of New York · *Sharon and Darren* · **Nigel Gray**
The Thing-in-a-Box · **Diana Hendry**
Desperate for a Dog · *Houdini Dog* · *More Dog Trouble* · **Rose Impey**
Georgie and the Computer Bugs · *Georgie and the Dragon* ·
Georgie and the Planet Raider · **Julia Jarman**
Cowardy Cowardy Cutlass · *Cutlass Rules the Waves* · *Free With Every Pack* ·
Mo and the Mummy Case · *The Fizziness Business* · **Robin Kingsland**
Albertine, Goose Queen · *And Pigs Might Fly!* · *Jigger's Day Off* ·
Martians at Mudpuddle Farm · *Mossop's Last Chance* · **Michael Morpurgo**
Granny Grimm's Gruesome Glasses · **Jenny Nimmo**
Grubble Trouble · **Hilda Offen**
Hiccup Harry · *Harry Moves House* · *Harry's Party* · *Harry with Spots On* ·
Chris Powling
Grandad's Concrete Garden · **Shoo Rayner**
The Father Christmas Trap · **Margaret Stonborough**
Our Toilet's Haunted · **John Talbot**
Pesters of the West · **Lisa Taylor**
Jacko · *Lost Property* . *Messages* · *Rhyming Russell* · **Pat Thomson**

First published in Great Britain by
A & C Black (Publishers) Ltd 1995
First published by Collins in 1995
10 9 8 7 6 5 4

Collins is an imprint of HarperCollins*Publishers* Ltd
77-85 Fulham Palace Road, London W6 8JB.

Text copyright © 1995 Brough Girling
Illustrations copyright © 1995 Tony Blundell

ISBN 0-00-675001-X

Printed in Great Britain by Clays Ltd, St Ives plc

Chapter One

Do you like chocolate biscuits?

I love them! Most dogs do.

And this is Police Officer Sally Jenkins – the officer who looks after me (actually I look after her).

Extra special police dog hat

Sharp Eyes

Head on one side for extra appeal

Collar with police number on

Extra special Waggy Tail

One morning when we arrived at the police station, there was a note for Sally from Chief Inspector Johnson.

> Dear Officer Jenkins,
> Meet me in my office at 9:30 a.m.
> I want to introduce you to
> a new member of the police
> force who could change
> your life!
>
> Chief Inspector.

I don't know why, but whenever the
Chief Inspector asks to see Sally, it
always sends her into a terrible
panic. I can't understand it myself.
I'm sure he just wants to
congratulate us on our excellent
police work.

While we waited in his office for the Chief Inspector to arrive, Sally had a cup of tea to calm her nerves, and I had a chocolate biscuit.

9

I don't know if you've discovered the best way to eat chocolate biscuits? What you do is turn all of them chocolate side up first (use your nose to do this), and then lick off all the chocolate from each one. Yummy! This way you don't have to bother with all the boring old biscuit underneath.

I think Sally was just going to speak
to me about something when Chief
Inspector Johnson arrived.

11

NORA BONE'S GUIDE TO PARTS OF THE HORSE

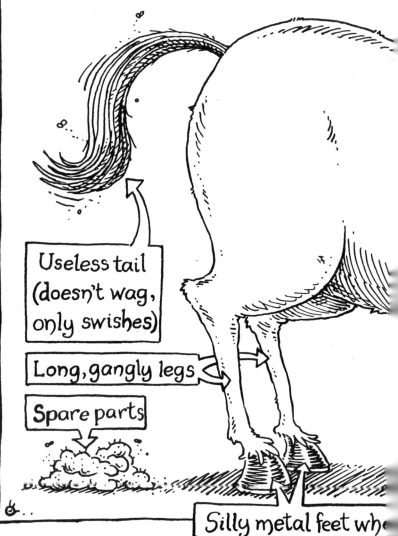

Useless tail (doesn't wag, only swishes)

Long, gangly legs

Spare parts

Silly metal feet wh

15

All horses are stupid, but this one takes the biscuit! (Just my little joke . . .)

19

Chapter Two

Not many minutes later we were
getting out of Sally's police car,
outside number 57 Oak Tree Drive.
The Potter family were standing on
their front step waiting for us.

While Sally spoke to the family,
I decided to go inside the house
and do a bit of police investigating
of my own.

The first thing I decided to
investigate was the Potters' cat.

I was just about to catch it when I
had a bit of bad luck.

I suddenly thought it would be a
good idea to stay upstairs for a little
while. So I hid under Jennifer's bed.

Have you ever had the feeling that there's something spooky under your bed?

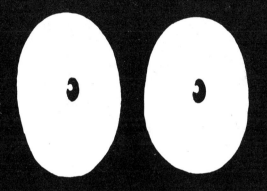

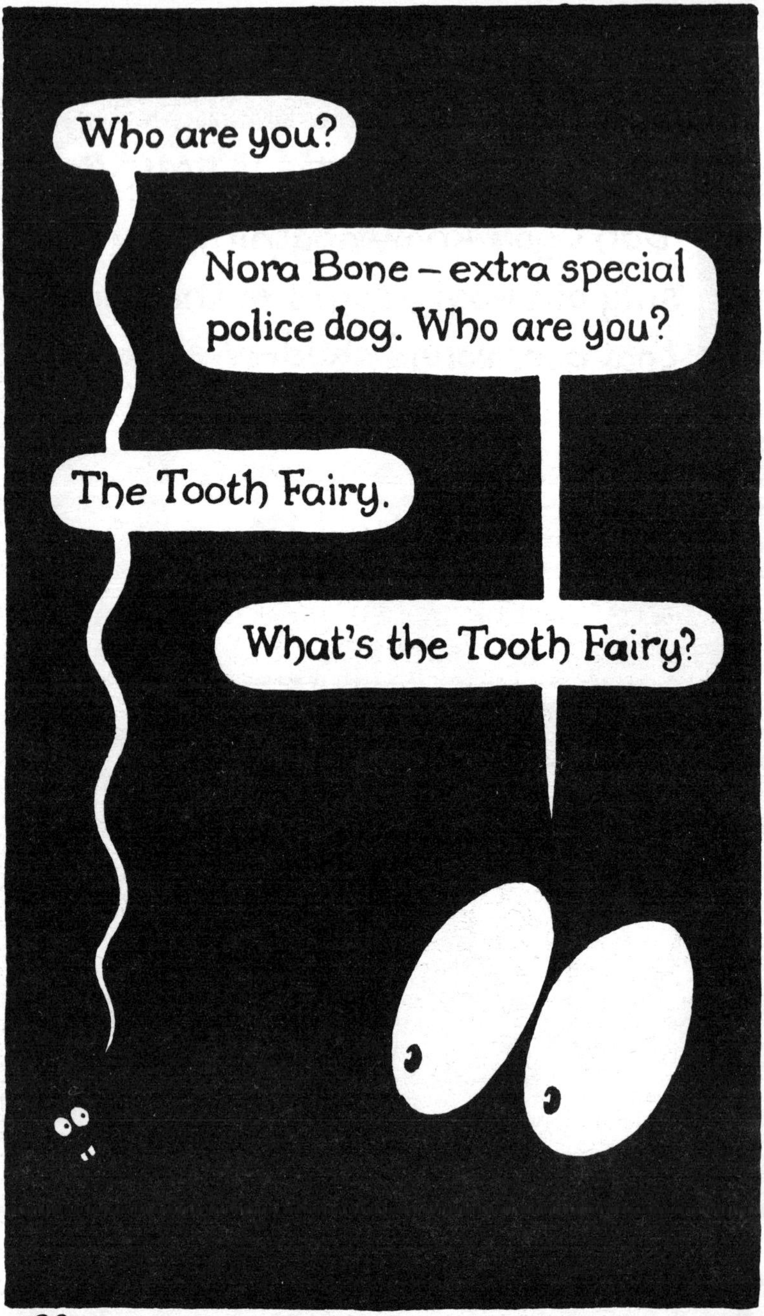
Who are you?
Nora Bone – extra special police dog. Who are you?
The Tooth Fairy.
What's the Tooth Fairy?

This sounded a bit daft to me, but to be polite I asked her what she did with all the teeth.

Why it's simple silly! I thread them on cobwebs to make pearly necklaces for our Fairy Queen, or use them for stepping stones – so that elves and goblins can cross the sparkling streams in fairyland!

This Tooth Fairy is as nutty as a peanut butter sandwich. Totally loopy!

Quite right, Nora. She's as loopy as a shoelace of licorice.

I reckoned it was time to get on with some police investigating work, so I asked her what she was doing under Jennifer Potter's bed . . .

Well, I'd just come to give her a coin for a dear little front tooth she lost yesterday, when I had a most frightening experience.

I'd collected the tooth from under Jennifer's pillow and was just going downstairs to fly out through the letterbox – that's how we usually come and go – when I heard the sound of breaking glass.

The next moment two terrible
rough men came up the stairs!
I flew into the front bedroom,
thinking I might be able to get out
through a window. But imagine my
horror when I realised that they
were coming into the bedroom
too . . . I nearly wet my knicks!

I was so frightened that as I landed on the top of Mrs Potter's dressing-table mirror, near the window, I dropped Jennifer's dear little tooth!

I looked down and saw it land on the dressing-table and then it bounced into a small open drawer. It landed next to a lovely little pearl bracelet. But there was nothing I could do about it because of the two horrible men!

I hid behind the mirror and watched in horror as one of them crept over to the dressing-table, pulled out the drawer, and put it under his arm!

The other one picked up a lady's watch and some money and put it in his pocket!

When they went downstairs again, I looked  through the bannisters and saw them pick up lots of other things.

I saw them climb out of the living-room window, and a moment later, they both got on to a small girl's bike and pedalled off on it.

I was so frightened that they might come back that I dashed back up here as fast as my tiny wings would carry me! I hid under the bed in case they'd seen me. Oh, I was so scared – and I've snagged my tights and lost the precious tooth.

Whatever will the Fairy Queen say?

Sob!

Sob!

?

I didn't have time to think about the question because I heard Sally's voice. I think she was trying to attract my attention.

NORA! NORA BONE! WHERE ARE YOU, YOU WRETCHED DOG?! COME HERE AT ONCE! HEEL! WICKED DOG! HEEL!!

It was obvious that Sally needed me downstairs, but I wasn't going anywhere without little Fairy Features. Loopy as she was, she'd seen the whole thing.

So we set off down the stairs.

When we got outside,
dear old Sally
was ever so talkative . . .

Look you stupid dog! That family has lost money and jewellry and other valuables because of a burglary; poor young Jennifer's bike's been stolen too, and all you do to help is chase their cat, knock over potted plants and ruin their hall carpet! I've a good mind to drop you off at the Dogs' Home!!

But I wasn't really listening to her – I was looking at the large crowd of neighbours who had gathered to see how a daring and efficient police dog goes about its duties!

Police dogs are trained to act
quickly, so I acted quickly . . .

Chapter Three

I didn't have time to see if Sally was
joining in the hunt, but I could hear
her shouts of encouragement
behind me.

NORA BONE!
Come back here you stupid animal!
Stop! Come here at once!!!!
Wretched dog, **THIS WAY!!!**

I was soon going flat out – much faster than any horse could have managed. The loopy little Tooth Fairy seemed quite impressed!

Oh my golly! Oh my gosh! I think I might just be going to be a little bit sick....!!!

By this time I was way ahead of Sally.

She's only got two legs, so she runs a bit slower than I do!

I expect she's so far behind that she's stopped for a chat or a little rest!

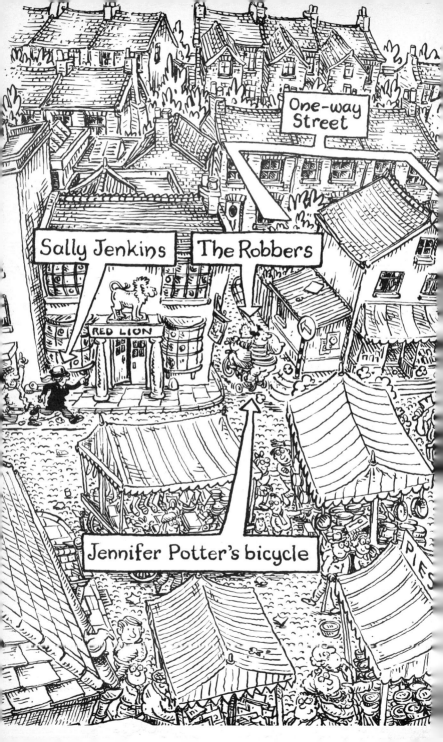

One-way Street

Sally Jenkins

The Robbers

RED LION

Jennifer Potter's bicycle

PIES

Lost them ...... pant pant...
which way ..... pant pant...
did they go?
SKIDDD!!
I don't know. I didn't see...

I must admit, *pant*
that at this point, *pant*
I was feeling, *pant*
a bit puffed. *pant*

pant
pant

a spare pair of pants — (my little joke!)

Then I saw them . . .

...SAUSAGES !!!!

What happened next took me a bit
by surprise . . .

59

I've changed my mind about horses, Jenkins. Unreliable creatures. Very dangerous. Forget the riding lessons. Dogs are better – look at the way Nora here did that trick with the sausages. It was her quick thinking that lead to the arrest of those horrible criminals. Well done! You have both won a medal and the big reward for their capture! Have a biscuit!